OSO

Greek Stories

Retold by Robert Hull
Illustrated by Adam Stower and Claire Robinson

Wayland

Tales From Around The World

African Stories
Egyptian Stories
Greek Stories
Native North American Stories
Norse Stories
Roman Stories

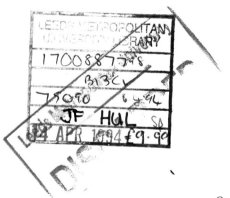
Editor: Kate Asser
Series Editor: Catherine Ellis
Series Designer: Tracy Gross
Book Designer: Mark Whitchurch
Consultant: Dr. Angus Bowie, The Queen's College, Oxford
Colour artwork by Adam Stower
Black and white artwork by Claire Robinson
Map on page 47 by Peter Bull

First published in 1993 by
Wayland (Publishers) Ltd
61 Western Road, Hove
East Sussex BN3 1JD, England

British Library Cataloguing in Publication Data

Hull, Robert
Greek Stories. – (Tales
from Around the World Series)
I. Title   II. Series
292.13

ISBN 0-7502-0792-2

Typeset by Dorchester Typesetting Group Ltd
Printed in Italy by G. Canale & C.S.p.A., Turin

Contents

Introduction   4
Circe   6
Midas and His Gold Touch   18
A Duel of Tunes   24
Arachne   30
Orpheus   38
Notes   47
Further Reading   48

Introduction

Have you ever heard someone say 'If looks could kill . . .'? Well, in one Greek story, the tale of the Gorgon Medusa, looks could kill. Hers did – one glance, and you were stone. Every time we say, more than two thousand years later, 'If looks could kill . . .', our minds are taking a quick dip into a Greek story. Do you ever make a 'titanic' effort? When you do, you're like a giant god, a Titan. If you ever feel 'panic', it's because the god Pan has crept up to give you a scare.

Greek stories are all around us. We might not recognize them, but we meet them every day, in our language. That sound coming back to you in a whispering gallery or an alleyway is the voice of Echo, a nymph who, as a punishment, could not speak her own words, but only repeat the words of others.

At night, Greek stories circulate above our heads, in the stars. The Great Bear, near the north pole, is a story about a young woman called Callisto, who was changed into a bear by Hera, the wife of the chief god Zeus. Hera was furious at Zeus for falling in love with Callisto. After Callisto died, Zeus put her in the stars, to live for ever and be admired from earth. The ancient Greek word for bear – *arktos* – is now in our language, in the word 'Arctic'.

The world of the Greeks was as crammed full of stories as the sky is with stars. Forests, mountainsides, rivers, streams, the air, the sea, were full of beings having adventures. There were the gods from Olympus, like Zeus and Athene, with magical powers –

becoming invisible and then appearing out of nowhere. There were local gods, like the river gods with long, flowing beards. There were beautiful nymphs of the mountains and the sea-shore who lived for thousands of years. There were dogs with three heads, and serpents with fifty. There were the wise Centaurs, half-horse and half-human, and ugly satyrs with goat bodies. A lot could happen in this crowded world, and it nearly always did.

The Greek gods loved taking part in others' lives. It was easy for them; they could take on whatever disguise they wanted, and turn other beings into different shapes as well. This often happened when they were angry. Once, when a passing goddess (in disguise) was refused a drink from a pond, a villageful of people was changed into a pondful of frogs!

The gods may have had supernatural powers, but they also behaved like humans. They fell in love, sometimes with ordinary people, they got angry and mean, or were kind and loyal – like people. Above all else Greek stories are about people. There are well-known characters, men and women with great, 'god-like' skills – Orpheus with his music and Arachne with her weaving. But there are also ordinary people, like Baucis and Philemon, whose kindness is remembered. In other places you can read about the courage of Antigone, the daring of Icarus, and a hundred more characters whose fascinating stories have been told over and over.

Who were they, these people who told so many stories, these ancient Greeks? By about 700 BC they lived in what is now Greece, and on the western coast of Turkey. Later they started spreading west, to Sicily, Italy, and beyond. They took with them things they had made. They were amazing makers of temples, paintings, vases, plays, sculptures, games, science, boats, cities, geometry, poetry, arguments, ideas, words. Some things have come down to people like us, who watch their plays, see their sculptures, do their geometry and think with their ideas without realizing.

And read their stories. The spread of their stories is a story itself, something magical. But Greek stories are magical even when they have no magic in them.

5

Circe

When Helen, the beautiful wife of Menelaus, the Greek king of Sparta, was stolen away to Troy by Paris, who was one of the sons of King Priam of Troy, a war began between the Greeks and Trojans that lasted ten years. Greek armies sailed to Troy to bring back Helen; they camped outside its walls, and fought, and waited. Eventually, the Greeks burned down Troy itself, and Helen went back to Sparta with Menelaus. At the end of the war, some of the Greeks sailed home easily, some never returned. Odysseus, the most famous of the Greek chieftains, trying to find his way back home to the island of Ithaca, was hindered by Poseidon, god of the sea. Odysseus had blinded Poseidon's son, Polyphemus, the one-eyed giant. It was ten years before Odysseus, having lost all the men who had started back with him from Troy, arrived in Ithaca again – and only then after some amazing and terrifying adventures. Perhaps the strangest of them took place on the island of Aeaea, home of the witch-goddess, Circe.

Odysseus found himself, yet again, lying exhausted on the sandy beach of an island he didn't recognize. They had been so near home. They had even seen, in the distance, the beacon-lights that always glimmered on the cliffs of Ithaca. And then . . .

Odysseus was fond of his few remaining men, but that didn't stop him thinking that for half the time, when they weren't being brave, helpful heroes, they

could act like idiots. Greedy idiots they had been this time, thinking there was treasure stowed in the hold, in the bag with the silver chain round its neck. Fancy thinking about money and treasure when they had been away from their island home for twenty years, and the actual lights of its cliff-tops were visible, twinkling in the distance.

Odysseus cursed himself again for having relaxed even for an instant. The rest of his ships sunk, so many men drowned or eaten, all because he had allowed himself a few minutes' sleep while someone else looked after the rudder . . .

For years Poseidon had blown them all over the place, from island to island, west towards home, south towards Africa, back towards Troy. Then finally the Wind-King, Aeolus, had given Odysseus a huge bag, with a silver chain bound tightly round the neck, in which were imprisoned all the winds that might blow Odysseus off course on the last stretch of his journey home. And what did his idiot crew do? They suspected

him of piling up treasure for his return and, in the few crucial minutes while he was having a rare doze, they broke the silver chain and started to open the bag, just to see what was in there.

They found out quicker than they expected. The trapped winds, all the wrong ones, rushed out in a howling whoosh. There was a thump as one by one the sails of the boats flapped full. Odysseus snapped awake and thought for a moment they'd hit land. Off the boats went at a foaming gallop, slewing hard round to face south, in the opposite direction from Ithaca, and batting about almost out of control in the flapping fury of the winds that had been let out of the bag.

They were blown straight back to the floating island kingdom of Aeolus. The Wind-King refused to have anything to do with them this time, and they had to put to sea again without a wind. They rowed for six days and nights, with only casual breezes to help, then at last they reached land. But what a place they had come to – the land of the Laestrygonian giants! From near the beach Odysseus had seen a wisp of smoke in the distance, so he and a party of men went to find out who lived there. They discovered soon enough, at the house of the chief. The Laestrygonian giants ate people, and without so much as a 'good afternoon' they pounced on several of Odysseus' men and started to champ them down. Preoccupied with eating, they watched stupidly over the top of their meal and let Odysseus and his remaining uneaten men escape.

A few minutes later the giants followed, galloping right down to the sea. Odysseus' boats were now launched, but were still near the cliffs. The giants, tearing off huge rocks and hurling them down from above with thunderous shouts, sank all of the boats but one, and then harpooned the drowning men with heavy arrows tied to long ropes. Only Odysseus, with a handful of men in the one boat, escaped. They had somehow reached this new island, where they had now collapsed on the beach for two days and nights in utter exhaustion.

And so here Odysseus was, wherever 'here' was. Never before, travelling the deserted wastes of the seas, had he been truly lost.

8

Odysseus lay on the sand watching the sun shift upwards through the leaves of an olive tree, and decided he had better make a move. The rest of his men were still dead to the world.

After an hour's climb from the beach he came to a small rock which made a good view-point. The island looked small and deserted, but as his gaze travelled the horizon a second time, he saw, in the distance, a thin column of smoke. They were not alone.

He hurried back. While he had been gone, the men had roused themselves and made a fire. One of them had even shot a small deer, which was already turning on a spit and filling the cool air with the extra scent of breakfast roast. When Odysseus told them that he had seen some smoke in the distance, there were cries of alarm. Perhaps they were back on the island of the giants! But Odysseus calmed them. From his view-point he had seen the shape of the whole island, and knew they had never before set foot on it.

While they were eating, Odysseus gazed out to sea, longingly north towards Ithaca, thinking of a plan. His years of wandering had taught him caution, and he decided that half of his few men would stay to guard the boat, and half would explore. They drew lots to divide the crew. It was agreed that Odysseus and his group would stay, and that Eurylochus, his second-in-command, would take the other half and find out where the smoke was coming from.

After breakfast Eurylochus and his men trooped off uphill, while Odysseus and the others either lay in the shade round the boat or went for a swim.

It was not till late in the afternoon that Eurylochus, and only Eurylochus, returned. His face was as grey as the ship's sail.

'Odysseus, this is no island for men. This is an island where nightmares wander freely. Let us leave it behind and sail on, even though we don't know where we are. Only horror can drop anchor here. This island . . .'

'Eurylochus, what are you raging about? What have you seen? Tell me calmly.'

'What I have seen! – what have I not seen? I have seen men who . . .'

'Tell me calmly, from the beginning.'

'First we saw the column of smoke, then we went through the forest till we found where it came from.'

'Where was that?'

'A small palace, a mansion. There was no one around, and the gates were open, so we stood in the entrance, wondering whether to go on. There was a voice from inside the palace – a woman singing – and the sound of a loom, that quiet, clattery noise. Then, as we were standing there, guess what just came trotting round the corner of the house, large as life . . . guess . . .'

'I can't imagine. Another Cyclops?'

'A wolf, a huge, grey wolf. And before anyone had time to fit an arrow to a bowstring it reared up and had its paws on my shoulders. I tried to grab its throat but it was licking my face and whining. I have never been so frightened in my life, and it was looking at me with this expression, not like an animal, there was something human in its eyes. Then it slipped down and nuzzled round my ankles. Two more creatures had come up, a bear and a lion. They moved like a real bear and lion, but there was no look of bear or lion in those eyes. The bear put its muzzle over one of the men's shoulders and gave him a gentle hug, and the lion licked another one's knees, gently, because lions have rough tongues.'

Odysseus was looking hard at Eurylochus. 'This isn't a good time to joke, Eurylochus. I suppose the rest are hiding round the corner and holding their faces like bags of wind, trying not to laugh.'

'Odysseus, I swear. What I'm saying is true. We must get off this island now. We must have been to more weird places than any sailors in history, but this is the worst. It's Weirdland itself.'

A few minutes ago Odysseus had been thinking longingly of home. Now he was seething with curiosity. He had to find out what was going on. Odysseus always needed to find out. He could never leave a good mystery alone. Then he realized he had forgotten about the others.

'What about the rest of the men?'

'This is the awful part. It was horrible. While we were staring at these weird animal creatures, a woman came out. The singing had stopped, so maybe it was her. She was beautiful, I tell you, the most beautiful woman I've seen since we left Greece all those years ago.'

'Including Helen?'

'Including Helen.'

12

Odysseus was even more curious. 'Then?'

'She had this really low, musical voice, "How marvellous," she said, "to have visitors suddenly appear from nowhere at the gates of my lonely little palace. Please, come in, take some refreshment. You look utterly exhausted." And she turned this slow, gorgeous smile on the men and said, "Come, you poor things, follow me. You have come far. Stay and rest. Have a little luxury. Have a change." And they just followed her. Without a word to me they all trooped in behind her, with the animal creatures trailing after. I don't know why, but I didn't feel like it. It was the animals for one thing – they'd gone all quiet and still when she came out – and she definitely gave me the creeps too, even though she was beautiful. Never mind that super-charmer smile and her saying how pleased she was, I don't think she was a bit surprised to see us. She knew the men would go inside the moment she suggested it. I don't know why I know, it's just the feeling I had that it was all planned.'

'You were still outside?' asked Odysseus.

'I faded off round the corner when they went in. I didn't know whether to run, or try to see what was going on. There was a window, and I crept along the wall to see in. It was very rich-looking in there. Beautiful tables and couches, piles of food, drink in silver jugs. The animals were sprawled round as well. They were sort of watching, as if they were waiting for something. The men were having their feet washed by these beautiful girls, you should have seen their faces. Then the queen, or whoever she is, went round with some drink for them. She poured it herself from a gold bowl. "Now," she says, "Welcome, strangers. Here's to your health and comfort. Drink! To this surprising luxury and comfort, and a really marvellous change. Drink to me, Circe, your benefactress." So they did, even though they weren't sure what a benefactress was. Well, that's the last toast they'll drink, I tell you.'

'What do you mean?'

'They're pigs now.'

'Pigs?!'

'Pigs. She changed them into pigs with her drink. "Welcome, my wallowers!" she sings. "Peace, precious

13

porkers! Feed, my fond favourites! Afterwards a little snooze, my silky snouts." It was horrible. And there they were, grunting round and dropping their snouts into the gold dishes and squealing away just like real pigs. Then they all flopped down and snored like the sea. Now do you believe me? Now will you tell me that we can leave straightaway?'

'We cannot leave.' Odysseus' expression was hard and angry. Without another word he took up his bow and his sword. Eurylochus was too scared to be a useful companion on a second expedition, so Odysseus set out on his own.

On top of the hill again, as he watched the smoke drifting upwards, Odysseus wondered what he could do to combat the enchantments of Circe. Attack with his men? Burn down her palace?

Into the middle of his thoughts came a clap of wings, and there before him was Hermes, the gods' messenger.

'Listen to me, Odysseus. You cannot combat Circe, that hater of human beings, unaided, so I have come to give you my help. Look.' He gave Odysseus a small white flower with a black root. 'Take this moly, the flower the gods cull, into the palace of Circe. Accept her welcome when she summons you in. She will offer you food and drink. Accept all she offers, but remember – so that you will not follow your men on another wasted journey into the body of a pig – remember to savour the scent of this flower before you drink her poisons. No more than that. She will drink with you and then order you to a sty. Then you must take out your sword and threaten her, and overpower her enchantment.' And off Hermes sped, without another word, back towards Olympus.

When Odysseus arrived at the palace porch, he called out. Circe herself came to the doors, and invited him in. He was taken into her sumptuous apartment in the centre of the palace, where young women were preparing all sorts of herbs and spiced drinks.

Circe came to him with a golden bowl, and pouring out a dark, ruby liquid into a silver cup, then sitting by him, invited him to drink. As he reached for the cup with one hand, he inhaled the scent of the flower concealed in the other. He drank. Circe sprang up with a wild glint in her eye.

'Off you go, wandering pig, to your sty. No more spacious seas for you. Just watch the little waves your snout makes in your trough! Off you go, off!'

The hands of Odysseus kept their five fingers, his hair retained its blackness. Circe stared at him. 'Who are you?'

'I am the far-famed Odysseus,' Odysseus roared at her, standing and drawing his sword, 'a man who intends to stay a man, even in your perverted palatial pig-hole!'

Circe continued to gape in disbelief. Then something dawned on her, a memory, a long-ago prophecy that someone had made about a great traveller on his way home from the Troy wars. A man who would defeat her magic malice. This must be the man, this Odysseus, whose name means 'suffering'.

'You are the one!' was all she could gasp out, and she sank down into the couch, gazing at Odysseus as if she were in love with him already. 'You are the one. Stay with me. Sit with me here and tell me your story. Stay with me.'

But Odysseus, the wiliest of rulers, knew too well the unruly wiles of women witch-goddesses. 'How often do you say that, Circe, to the travellers you trap here?'

'Never till now have I spoken such words.'

'Prove yourself, then. Give me back my men as proof.'

'Will you stay then? And love me?'

'Perhaps.'

Circe smiled. 'Sit by me.' She turned to one of her girls. 'Bring them.'

A minute later and seven pigs came trotting in, snouts trailing the marble floor, snuffling hopefully. With a surge of pity Odysseus saw his men, imprisoned in the bodies of pigs, come crowding round him, grunting gently and squeaking, looking up at him with pink human eyes.

Circe stood up, and went amongst the pigs scattering drops of a coloured liquid over each one of them. They suddenly went quiet, then an amazing change took place. First their wide snouts became thinner, then their hairy bristles began to drop off so fast the floor was like a forest path scattered with pine needles. Then they rose on their hind legs like dogs. Their excited squealing and grunting began to include bits of words: 'Onk-onk-eus! Onk-yss-eus.'

When they were men again, they stood there examining their shoulders and arms and legs, peering into polished silver cups and dishes and feeling their re-discovered ears and noses. Odysseus felt even more sorry for them than he had ever done on all their long wanderings. In that moment Odysseus decided they would stay on Circe's island for a while. They needed a rest from the thunder of the heaving sea. He did too.

It was a whole year before they departed. The enchantment that Circe finally worked on Odysseus was not her magic, only herself.

17

Midas and His Gold Touch

*H*uman beings who get mixed up with the gods have to be careful. They need to have their wits about them. Gods need to be paid the right amount of respect.

Keeping his wits about him was one thing King Midas was no good at. When he needed them most, they deserted him. It would have been much better if he'd kept them nearby when he met a god.

Everyone knew Midas was going to be rich, even when he was a baby. One day a procession of ants was seen carrying some grains of wheat up his cradle and placing them on his lips. The soothsayers said it meant that great wealth was coming to him. It did. Midas became rich, the owner of great estates and famous rose gardens.

One day some of Midas' peasants told him they had found a drunk old man sprawled asleep in the roses. It was true. When Midas came out he saw for himself – a red-faced old man sprawled asleep against the wall in a sunny corner of his favourite rose garden, and a contented-looking ass tethered nearby.

What the peasants had said was true as far as it went, but there was more to it. The drunk old man snoring in the sun among the roses wasn't just any drunk old man. It was the nearly-god Silenus, son of one god, Pan, and philosopher and friend of another god, Dionysus. In other words, a drunk old man with divine connections, and worth treating well.

18

One of the peasants realized who Silenus was just in time, so they didn't shake him awake, though Midas, who didn't think the old man looked very goddish or philosophical lying there drunk, was doubtful until he heard Silenus' first words.

'Where am I? Where's Dionysus and the rest? Who are you lot? They've just dumped me!'

It wasn't true, as it turned out. Silenus hadn't been abandoned, he'd fallen asleep on his donkey, which had stopped for a long, luxurious nibble on the leaves of an olive tree. While Dionysus and the rest of his followers kept steadily on with their journey, Silenus and donkey had fallen behind, and by the time Silenus woke up there was no way of telling where the rest had gone. Realizing he was lost, Silenus decided, like a true philosopher, to go to sleep again, but properly this time, in a nice shady corner of the rose garden.

Silenus explained all this to Midas back in his mansion.

'Well, what are we to do?' said Midas, who was never the first with a brilliant idea.

'Perhaps, er, perhaps we ought to take a little refreshment?' suggested Silenus. 'To help us think clearly. A bit of wine even? I find I grow wiser with wine.'

'But of course,' Midas said, and ordered a servant to bring a jug of wine. Silenus was, after all, the chief companion and tutor of the god of wine, who was also partial to a bit of honey, milk and so on, and it wouldn't do to appear grudging or slow in providing any of these things.

'A little honey, too? Milk?'

'No thank you, no, I can focus better on just one article at a time.'

Midas had been thinking. 'What I wish, Silenus, is that you would honour us with your presence for some few days,' he said. 'That is, if keeping you here would not appear disrespectful to the god Dionysus, your patron.'

Silenus noticed that Midas was trying hard to say the right thing, and thought that if Midas was so keen to have him to stay, he might receive very god-like treatment indeed, particularly in the wine department.

As far as Dionysus was concerned, Silenus was thinking that by entertaining him, Midas was really entertaining Dionysus, who ought to be pleased.

'Very well, though it interrupts my journey somewhat. Since you wish to honour the great god Dionysus in this way, I consent. I will stay.'

Midas wasn't sharp enough to notice that Silenus was laying it on rather thick. He couldn't see Silenus was being a real old sham. He was just delighted. So for ten days Silenus had a splendid time, and at the end of his stay Midas sent some of his servants to act as guides to Silenus on his journey back to Dionysus.

Dionysus was relieved to see his friend and teacher again. He was also pleased that Midas had shown such respect, through Silenus the nearly-god, to himself Dionysus, the real god. He sent word to Midas that, as a reward, he wished to offer him some great gift. What object or skill would Midas like to possess? He could have anything he wanted.

Midas was overwhelmed. Such a message from a god! What should he ask for? What was the most wished-for thing he could think of? What did everyone want most?

'Let me think,' he thought. 'Health? No, I have that. Brains? No, I've got enough of those. Great skill at something? No, I can't think of anything I need to be really good at.'

Suddenly he had it. Gold! That was it! No one he knew ever said they had had enough. Even the wealthiest people couldn't afford this or that. He needed more gold. Gold, gold, gold! Lots of it. Gold all round him, gold all the time! A blinding thought struck him. As his gift from Dionysus he would ask that all the things he touched would be gold.

Off went the messenger, and a few days later back he came.

'The god says, do you wish for all the things you touch to be gold? Really?'

'I do.'

'The god says he will grant your wish, whatever it is, exactly as he said, exactly as you asked. Is this what – exactly – you wish for? Do you solemnly wish – I repeat – for everything you touch to be gold?'

Midas couldn't help thinking 'What's the fellow fiddle-faddling about for?' and said, 'Yes, yes, I solemnly do.'

'Very well. You have your wish.' And the messenger just left.

'Is that it, then?' thought Midas. 'Right, let's start. How do I start?' He was frantically excited. All he had to do to make gold was – touch something. 'What? Did it matter? What first? How about this dented old wine-cup?' He reached for it and held it. A sort of sudden pins-and-needles-y tingle passed through his hand, and suddenly there he was, holding a gold wine-cup, still a bit dented. 'But', he thought with a giggle, 'dented bronze cups and dented gold cups are a bit different, aren't they?'

22

'Now, what shall I drink from my dented old gold cup? I know, a toast to Dionysus, in thanks. A little wine.' So, he picked up a jug of wine – tingle across his hand – which was already a gold jug by the time it was pouring wine into his gold cup.

'To Dionysus! All hail! All . . . Aargh . . . ugh . . . !'

Midas was enjoying his first mouthful of cold gold wine-that-wasn't-wine any more and was coughing and splurting it out and about in little gold explosions.

When his mouth had calmed down Midas sat for a few minutes thinking, not touching anything. He began to wonder if there was a hitch in his new gold world. Surely not everything he touched would . . . not everything, not certain things, like . . . food? Other people . . . ? If he embraced them would he have gold friends? Were gold friends any use? Perhaps he could send to Dionysus to have the wish altered a bit, so that he could have all the gold things he wanted without any of the inconvenience. Just object things, things like this table – tingle – of gold, and these heavy curtains of – tingle – gold. He was a millionaire already, in five minutes!

Midas hadn't fully understood yet, but later that day, when he became really hungry and really thirsty, he did. It was when he found the supper menu was gleaming cold, gold chop, gold olives to crack the teeth on, gold milk to spit out in despair.

Dionysus had known what would happen, and because Midas had treated Silenus so well and brought him back, he had already sent his servant to advise Midas what to do.

To escape the curse of his stupid wish, Midas had to go far from his rich estate to the poor country district where the River Pactolus sprang from the earth. Midas had to immerse himself in the gushing spring, unwish his wish, and ask for forgiveness from the unchanging waters.

For a while, as Midas stood in the throbbing source of the river, the water flowing past him became streaked with gold. Then gradually it turned sparklingly clear again.

Midas was cured of his terrible wish, but to this day people find gold in the bed of the River Pactolus.

A Duel of Tunes

After he was cured of turning everything to gold, Midas seemed a changed man. He scorned his wealth and spent all his time wandering about in the country, 'close to nature', as he used to say, watching the birds, looking at flowers and plants (not knowing anything much about them, though) and calling on the great god Pan: 'Oh Pan, Oh Pan, great Pan!' He sounded a bit dotty, to be honest.

He would wander all day in the forest, in a kind of daze, or on the mountain slopes, hoping for a glimpse of the goat-footed god, and listening out for the sound of his pipe. He knew people heard it sometimes on the hills, or in the forest at midday.

One day he was resting by a stream when he heard voices nearby. He crept along the bank, round the next bend, and came to a space by the water where Pan himself sat on a rock overlooking the river. He was playing his pipe to some nymphs of the river, trying hard to impress them. Midas was entranced by the music and the whole scene. After one little tune Pan said to his audience, 'My simple music is the kind everyone really prefers. Apollo's is too complicated and people only pretend they enjoy it. It's my pipe that plays the most real, natural music.' And he started again, with the nymphs, joined by doting Midas, in an admiring circle round him.

Apollo, god of music, heard Pan's pipe and he overheard his boastful prattle as well. He was indignant, and appeared in front of Pan with a few sharp words: 'Pan, your trills and whistles and runs may sound very haunting to the nymphs and simple humans who hear them by a stream in the forest or on the mountainside, with bird-sounds all round. They're like part of nature. But they are not like my music at all, which people come from far and wide to listen to for its own sake. They come to me to listen to the music of a god of music, not just to overhear the agreeable sounds of nature.'

Pan was furious, being spoken to like this in front of the lovely nymphs he'd spent months trying to get friendly with. There and then he challenged Apollo to a music competition. 'Apollo, snotty god of posh music, I suggest that we make music in single combat, in a stirring duel of tunes. My rural public, these charming nymphs, and that strange man who has just wandered by – all of them can vote. And Tmolus the mountain will be the final judge. He can take a detached view if anyone can.' They were actually on the slopes of Tmolus at that moment, and Pan was sure the mountain liked simple country tunes, and would be on his side. Of course the nymphs were bound to be.

'Very well,' Apollo replied.

'Agreed?' said Pan.

'Agreed.'

They would meet the next morning, on the mountainside, in the high, stony garden of Tmolus.

The next day Apollo came along dressed as he always did dress for a serious performance, in a long purple robe with gold clasps on his arms and round his ankles. He played for only a few minutes on his jewelled lyre. It was enough. The audience forgot where they were, and were so captivated that when he had finished they didn't applaud at once. They were silent, as the last few moments of music still flowed through them and died away in their minds. That few seconds' silence was the real applause, more than the clapping which followed it. Midas joined in the clapping, but only half-heartedly. The music wasn't cheerful enough, he thought; music should cheer you up, and make you want to march about.

Then it was Pan's turn. His music was tuneful in a happy, jerky, untidy sort of way, but in Tmolus'

25

garden, without the loud breeze backing it up in the trees, and the rhythmic sounds of the stream to help as well, it wasn't quite the same. Especially not after Apollo had just played to them. Even so, Midas nudged a nymph and said, 'Wasn't that lovely?'

Every single vote went to Apollo – except one. Midas thought Pan's music was much better for out-of-doors. But he didn't know quite what to say, except that he thought Pan's pipe sounded 'more exciting and interesting somehow' than Apollo's lyre.

You might have expected Apollo to be satisfied with that judgement, but he was very vain, and couldn't bear to think that any single member of his audience should prefer Pan. 'Exciting! Interesting! Pan's music better than my music!' he screamed. 'You no-tone stone-brain! You tuneless timber-ear! You've the hearing of an old, bored, deaf donkey, do you know that? In fact, you might just as well have donkey ears, to hear my music with. Here – a pair of appropriate ears!'

And at each side of his head Midas suddenly felt a tickle, then a strong tingle. Surely his ears couldn't be turning to gold? He grabbed them. They were big long hairy things! He ran down the mountain to the stream and looked in at his reflection. Long, hairy, donkey ears waved to him from deep in the water!

Back to his mansion went ass-eared Midas, keeping to the lonely paths and the dark forest. Once home, he managed to creep back inside without being seen. He wrapped his head in a huge bandage and called for his barber. He told him that he needed a new wig.

Next day the barber came with the wig, but to get it on Midas had to have his hair cut. He decided he would have to trust his barber with the awful secret, making him swear to tell no one, otherwise he'd die a nasty barbery death by one of his own razors.

The barber had promised, but there are some things that are very hard to keep to yourself. He'd sworn to tell no one, though, and he didn't. Instead, because he had to speak or burst, he went down to the river and whispered over the water, 'Midas has great long hairy donkey ears and I'm not telling anyone.' Home went the barber, relieved to be rid of his awful secret.

Once was enough. A silent reed at the river's edge heard every word, and with the smallest whisper nudged the next one. That reed bent over to the next. In no time the news of Midas' ears had spread amongst all the reeds. The musical words, 'Midas has great long hairy donkey ears,' passed from the whispering reeds to the talkative water, then to the leaves of the trees overhead, up the mountainside and over into the next valley. Soon the news was everywhere.

One day Midas noticed one of his servants looking hard at his wig . . .

Arachne

River nymphs, or naiads, are always young, and live for a very long time, perhaps thousands of years. They aren't gods, and have no amazing powers, but they protect rivers and look after them, just by being there. Naiads love wandering alongside water, and resting in the shade of trees at midday. They like to accompany the sounds of the river with their own humming and talking and singing, so when passers-by hear a stream rippling over the rocks, or water tumbling over a small fall, or the wind in the alders and willows, it is partly the river itself they hear and partly the nymphs. And when, as they like to, the naiads comb each other's hair, mend or weave clothes, swim, or dance, their easy movements pass into the water and the riverside trees.

River nymphs can hardly ever be lured from water. How strange then, one day, for villagers to see the watchful naiads who guard the waters of the beautiful River Pactolus leave the rocks and pools where they usually spend the afternoon swimming or lying in the shade, to walk to the dusty village nearby.

They were going to see another river. Inside one particular house in the village was a shady room where there was a woven river on the wall, a blue, glittering river that seemed to make the room pleasantly cool. It was another Pactolus, woven like their own designs. There, on the wall, was the pool they had just left, with the same water spilling over the rocks into it.

The room was in the house of Idon, a dyer of wool, who could make wool take many colours – scarlet, gold, green, and a rich purple that he made from the juices of the purple-fish. Idon had a daughter, Arachne, who since she was little had been fascinated by the bits of coloured wool she found on the floor of his workshop. She used to make simple pictures of houses and trees with them, laying the strands of wool on a table.

Soon Arachne had learned to use a weaving-frame, and started to weave pictures. She made tapestries of the things she saw round her – houses, trees, hills, rivers, flowers, birds, people – and of things she learned about from stories, even stories of the gods. From the first, Arachne's pictures were amazingly life-like, and villagers began to call at Idon's house just to see them.

The word spread, till Arachne's name was known in all the villages from the mountains to the coast. The daughter of a poor weaver from a village in the middle of nowhere became so famous that people made journeys of several days to see her pictures. And not only people. Whenever there was a river in a picture, as there often was, the ever-young naiads would come to look at it, wondering why they felt they could almost step into the water. Dryads, the nymphs of the forests, also came, and imagined they could hear the trees whispering in the wind on the slopes of the woven mountains.

There was even a rumour that sometimes the gods came in disguise to see how Arachne pictured them. Sometimes they liked what they saw, it was said, sometimes not, because in Arachne's pictures the gods could be vengeful, and treacherous. In paintings and sculptures they liked to seem heroic and splendid.

Arachne's work was so lifelike that birds which strayed indoors had been known to peck at the berries, and swallows had even tried to nest under the eaves of one of her houses. Dogs would bark at grazing sheep and, unless she was stopped, Arachne's cat would claw the woven birds.

On this particular morning, when the naiads had left the River Pactolus to visit Arachne, one of them said,

gazing at this other Pactolus, 'I believe that only Athene herself could have taught you. No other power could make this picture so like the real river we love and care for.'

She meant this to be a great compliment. It was like saying, 'Your skill is superhuman. It has come from the goddess herself.'

You'd think that anyone would be delighted by praise like that, but not Arachne. From the time when she would pick strands of dyed wool from her father's workshop floor and make simple shapes with them, she had thought only of how she herself, unaided and untaught, had made her own pictures.

'My skill comes from me. I taught myself,' she said.
The nymphs were startled.

'Surely no one . . .' one of them began to say.

'No one has taught me anything,' Arachne repeated. 'Unless it is my eyes that taught my hands, and my mind that taught my eyes.'

'And who taught your mind?' a nymph asked innocently.

'The mountains, the river, those trees. I look at them with my mind. You look at them. Now I have to work.'

She turned back to her weaving, and would say no more. The naiads left. As they went through the door, an old woman entered. Arachne did not recognize her. She had on a dusky, colourless cloak, and sandals that were scarcely holding together.

It was Athene herself, goddess of wisdom and skills –
pottery, house-building, shoemaking, soldiering and
many more, including weaving, which was a favourite
pastime. Athene was a very powerful goddess, and
could be dangerous; she once blinded a young man,
Teiresias, who happened to see her bathing naked. She
had overheard Arachne's boasting before, and had
come to see if Arachne really was claiming to be better
at weaving than herself . . .

Athene, in her disguise, praised Arachne's work just
as the river-nymphs had done. 'Anyone would think
you had learned your marvellous skill at Athene's
loom,' she said.

Arachne suspected nothing, but it was the second
time that morning that there had been mention of her
having a teacher, and it irritated her.

'I needed no teacher. No one has taught me
anything. I taught myself. If Athene herself came here,
I'd show her how I could weave pictures as beautiful
and full of life as hers, and maybe better. If she beat
me, she could weave my hair into a picture and throw
the rest away.'

'You would not be afraid of a contest with Athene
herself?' Athene asked.

'Of course not, can't you hear?'

'You are a very proud young woman, too proud for
your own good. You should ask forgiveness from
Athene for such thoughts.'

'Nonsense. I can think what I like, and she can come
when she likes.'

'She has already come,' Athene said, and the old
cloak and the old face vanished. A beautiful woman
stood there, as young as Arachne herself, with eyes,
Arachne immediately saw, of the same grey-blue that
she had woven into the morning sky above her river.

Arachne blushed and trembled at the sight of the
radiant goddess who took the place of the old woman
with the dusky cloak. All she could do was stammer,
'A-A-Athene . . .' She was suddenly frightened. Athene
smiled, and not kindly. The contest they had both
spoken of now had to begin. Arachne began to set up
a loom for herself, and had another arranged for
Athene to work on.

And so the two women, one an immortal goddess, one a mere human, began. A neighbour called in, word of the contest spread, and people came hurrying to watch. Only a few could fit into the room, so the rest stayed outside, eager to hear the reports sent out.

In the room they watched in awed silence as the goddess from Olympus and the young woman from the village fastened the separate vertical threads of the warp, and chose from amongst their amazing ranges of coloured threads the first ones to fit into the silver-headed shuttles. Soon the shuttles were flashing from side to side.

More slowly, the eyes went back and forth from picture to picture. They saw what looked like gold rain in Arachne's. Then they were drawn to a white mark in Athene's picture that slowly became a cloud-like smudge, which in half an hour had turned into a spring of water. Later the spring foamed out wider and somehow became the flowing mane of a horse.

Next to the standing horse there grew, thread by thread, a small olive tree.

The watchers turned to each other. They recognized the story of the naming of Athens, Athene's city. Athene was weaving a picture about herself, about the contest between herself and Poseidon, god of the sea, over which of their names should be used for the chief city of Attica. It showed both gods bringing a miraculous gift, and the people of Attica deciding which was the most valuable. Poseidon struck the sacred rock of the Acropolis, the highest point of the city, with his trident; a spring of salt water rushed out, and from its sparkling flow sprang the first horse. Poseidon's marvellous gift was the horse. In another part of the design Athene was hitting the same rock with her spear, and up there grew, in a second, an olive tree, the very first to grow anywhere. Athene's gift was judged more valuable, and so the city was called Athens.

Athene seemed to be reminding the watchers that she was one of the gods. And just in case they forgot how important the gods were, she added, one in each corner like warnings, four small pictures, stories of human beings who had offended the gods and been changed from their human shapes into wild creatures or inanimate things – a stork, a mountain, the stone steps of a temple.

Arachne's picture had many stories in it, mainly showing the ways the gods deceived human beings. Zeus was tricking Danaë into making love, throwing himself into her room as a shower of gold. Apollo, disguised as shepherd, was about to deceive a young girl, Issa. Though Athene's picture was amazingly life-like, Arachne's was more like life, more like the villagers' lives. The people watching loved it because it was full of sympathy for the deceived young women. Arachne's picture seemed to understand human life, Athene's flattered the gods.

The pictures were finished and it was time for the judgement. Athene went across to look at Arachne's, and Arachne went across to look at Athene's. Arachne found Athene's very accurate and interesting, but wasn't impressed by Athene telling a story about herself. It was showing off. As Athene looked at

Arachne's picture she felt a sudden anger. Her face blazed up like one of her woven sunsets. Her clenched knuckles showed white as the snow on Olympus. Some of the fury in her face was because the gods were not depicted as reverently as they should be, but most was there because she was looking at a picture every bit as skilled as her own, but with more life and energy in it.

In a frenzy of jealousy Athene tore at Arachne's loom, which keeled over with a splintering crash. She seized the sharp-headed shuttle, and hacked and stabbed at the picture, slashing it across again and again, until it was in shreds. Then she turned round towards Arachne herself, ready to do the same to her.

Arachne, grabbing the remains of her picture, fled out into the sunlight and ran and ran, down to the cool bank of the river. She sat for a while beneath an olive tree, in tears, unravelling all the threads of what was left of the picture. Then she twisted them into a thick, many-coloured rope, and in despair hanged herself from a branch.

But Arachne hadn't run far enough from Athene's rage, and she was unable to escape from her into death. Athene found her hanging there, still alive, and took her last revenge. 'Since you wish to hang, hang always. Since you wish to weave, weave always!' And she threw over Arachne some of the terrible, venomous juices that she had discovered while preparing her most gloomy dyes.

In the sunlight of the next morning, walking under the trees by the river, the nymphs of the Pactolus saw, draped over a bush, a strange woven design glistening with dew. The design was trembling, as if with fear. When a nymph touched one silver string of it, to calm it, a small creature ran to its edge and out of sight, as Arachne had run from Athene. It was the first web that Arachne, shrunk to a grey spider by jealous Athene, had spun in her new life.

The nymphs knew that only Athene, or perhaps Arachne, possessed such skill. Arachne was to spin and weave for the rest of time, but only the one design, with no gods or humans in it, and without the colour that had enchanted her as a child.

Orpheus

When Orpheus played his lyre on the mountainsides or in the forest, birds would stop singing and fly down to listen. Animals sprawled round him with their heads on their paws. That was how powerful and haunting his music was. When he travelled with Jason in the *Argo* on an expedition to find the Golden Fleece, dolphins often came to the bow of the boat to hear him; at night, when men were homesick round the fires on the beaches, they forgot their misery as they listened to him. Once, when a storm blew up, Orpheus took his lyre on deck and sang. As the music drifted across the water, the sea grew calm.

After the *Argo* returned, Orpheus married a sea-nymph, Eurydice, whom he had often seen at the edge of the sea, listening to him. At the marriage altar the torch flickered and smoked, and refused to burn properly, but no one except Orpheus noticed the unlucky sign, and he was too happy to worry about it.

For a while life was perfect. Like many lucky, newly married people they wanted to be on their own together, and were not very pleased when a friend of Orpheus, called Aristaeus, visited them without warning only days after the wedding. Aristaeus had invented a hive for keeping wild bees and gathering their honey, and intended to talk to Orpheus about the way his music drew creatures to him. Instead he fell in love with Eurydice.

38

One morning all three of them were walking on a path that led down through steep fields to the sea. Aristaeus pretended he wanted to show Eurydice some flowers that the bees liked, and Orpheus went ahead on his own. On the beach he looked out for his favourite dolphins, and listened to the always-changing musical sounds of the sea. After a while he began to wonder where Eurydice and Aristaeus were, and walked a little way back up the slope.

Seeing no sign of them, Orpheus started to run back up the path, and soon found Eurydice lying at one side of it, her face twisted with pain. She could hardly speak, but pointed to a small puncture mark at the side of her ankle, just above her sandal strap – a snakebite, with a small, smoky bruise round it.

Aristaeus had gone.

At the wedding, the torch had smoked, a sputtering trail of dark smoke instead of the bright flame that resembled the daylight. Orpheus remembered the omen, as he carried Eurydice home up the steep hill.

When she could speak, Eurydice told him that Aristaeus had violently thrown his arms round her, wanting to make love to her. She had twisted free, but as she ran, she stepped on a snake in the grass, which writhed its head back and bit her. Within hours of the bite Eurydice died, and descended into the world of the dead.

For days Orpheus could not speak, or bear to see anyone. He felt his life was over. In his imagination, he kept seeing Eurydice in their favourite places, walking with him in the fields, down at the sea's edge. Once he was sure he saw her shape ahead of him in the trees, and ran after her calling, 'Eurydice, Eurydice!' There was no one.

Orpheus slipped into black despair. He thought of only one thing, seeing her again.

He wanted to go down to the country of the dead. Singing his prayer on the lyre, he asked the oracle of the sacred oak of Zeus for the god's reply.

'Zeus who is everywhere,
in the crowded streets, in the marketplace,
in the quiet fields, along the singing sea-shore,
Zeus let me descend,
though I'm a living being,
down the steep paths of the Underworld
to find Eurydice in the shadows.'

In the rustling of the oak leaves Orpheus heard Zeus agreeing to his request, and so he started on his way to the Underworld. After a long journey he came to a country in the far west of the world, a country of continuous mists, where a grove of black poplars guards the entrance to the Underworld, where Hades and Persephone rule over the lands of the dead.

In the grove of poplars was a pair of bronze gates so high that they disappeared in mist. They were open, but the dark way through was blocked by the snarling and black-venomed slavering of Cerberus, Hades' watch-dog, a monster as big as the *Argo*, with three heads already baring their teeth and shrieking as loudly as the blacksmith god Hephaestus sawing into metal.

Orpheus sang to Cerberus the first song the monster had ever heard. The howling shrank to a confused whimper, then one after the other the heads sagged on to the huge paws. The six eyes grew calm, struggled to stay open, then one by one closed, and the beast finally slept.

There is a river nearby, called Acheron, which the souls of the dead have to cross to enter the Underworld. Charon was waiting, the ancient ferryman of the dead. Poling a rusty blue boat, he ferries endless cargoes of dead souls across the silent black water. Charon moves so slowly that his long, dirty beard, and the smelly cloak that spills from his bony shoulders, never sway an inch, but just hang there straight and still. His face is always in shadow, his empty eyes watch the water.

'I carry the dead, only the dead,' was all he said, in a throaty whisper, when Orpheus asked to be taken across. Orpheus touched the strings of his lyre, and sang. After a few moments Charon beckoned him aboard. As he poled the creaky boat across the slow, dark water he gazed at Orpheus, and for a few moments, as they crossed, the outline of his face was visible, the eyes glimmered as if he remembered something.

Orpheus stood on the far bank of Acheron. The shadows of many recently dead crowded round, wondering how a body still breathing could be visiting their silent land. They could not speak, they were already forgetting their lives on the earth. Orpheus peered round to see if he could see Eurydice, then walked on through them, playing a song made for her, about their short time together, hoping that she might hear it, and remember. He had to go to King Hades and Queen Persephone. The dead were their subjects, and no dead shadow had ever been given permission to return to the brightness of the sun and feel the fresh air; no one who had died had made a second journey with Charon.

But this was just what Orpheus intended to ask. He would ask the rulers of this silent land, where dark mists drifted endlessly, if he could take his wife back to the noisy, bright land of the living.

Seldom had a living being been seen in that place. The brightness that Orpheus carried with him made the spirits sick with new longing for the sun they still vaguely remembered. The music he played as he went rang out through the mists more strangely and clearly than the bells of goats on the hillside. But the music the dead heard seemed to be more than music. It was the most haunting that Orpheus had ever played. Its sounds seemed to recall the earth and its flowers and birds, the moods of the sea, rivers, the silence of the forest. As Orpheus passed, it stilled the spirits' useless longings.

Orpheus finally came to the black marble palace of Hades and Persephone. Hades and Persephone themselves might have been marble beings, they were so stiff and motionless on their high thrones, in long cloaks of purple and grey. Their faces were full of shadows, and their words of welcome seemed stilted and lifeless. Hades asked why he had come.

41

Orpheus answered by playing his lyre before them, and singing.

'I have come in hopeless love for my wife Eurydice. I hear that you yourselves were in love. Perhaps you remember what it was like. Perhaps you can imagine having love stolen from you. I beg you, by your own love that survives even in this terrible darkness, by these words that hang in the empty silence, to release her. We shall come back soon. But for a while let me have her again. We had hardly any time.'

Hades remembered his mad passion for Persephone. He had stolen her from the land above, from life. Persephone thought of the earth and the sun that she was still able to visit in the best time of the year. They looked at each other for a moment. Both of them were weeping.

All those who heard Orpheus were affected, even the spirits who suffered endless punishment for terrible crimes on earth. Tantalus, up to his neck in the pool that always emptied away when he bent to the water, for once found he could drink; he could take hold of the fruit which the wind always lifted just out of his reach. The wheel to which Ixion was lashed for trying to make love to the wife of Zeus, for once stopped. For the first and only time, the rock that Sisyphus pushed endlessly uphill didn't become too heavy near the summit and hurtle back down again to the bottom. For a while, the music of Orpheus had stopped even the worst tortures.

Persephone spoke: 'Eurydice can go with you. But there is a condition. Once you start climbing the path out of our kingdom, you must keep your gaze towards the bright world that Eurydice may return to. You must not turn round to look at her, to see if she is still following. You must only see her again by the light of day, when you have climbed out of here together.'

Then they summoned Eurydice, who came, still limping from her wound, and stood by Orpheus. He could not embrace a shadow, but had to content himself with gazing into her altered eyes.

And so they left, climbing the rocky path towards the light of day, Orpheus only a few yards ahead of his dead wife.

He had to trust that she was following. He couldn't turn to see that she had not fallen, and her floating steps could not disturb any stones, or make any sound on the winding rocky path.

Up and up they wound, through the same coiling dark mists, the same silence. Eurydice saw the darkest of the mists behind them, drifting below, at the edge of the Underworld. She could not tell how far they had come, but now she felt nearer light, and safety. She began to remember bits of the world again. Some of her remembering was painful – the path down to the sea, Aristaeus coming towards her. Then in her imagination she began to see other things clearly: stony beaches, rocks, blue seas, flowers at the cliff-edge.

Eurydice followed Orpheus, watching his steady step, seeing the mist spill round his shoulders. Though she was still a shadow, and would be till they reached the air, she understood what was happening more and more clearly as her mind began to return. She felt, like a cold touch, Orpheus' growing uncertainty, his confusion, his need to know if she was still there, behind him. She felt it more and more strongly. She urged him, silently, still to keep looking ahead.

As Orpheus climbed he felt more and more alone. Somehow he fought down his desire to just see her behind him on the path, but he kept thinking what an unforgettable moment of happiness it would be, just to see her there and know that they were going back to their house, their fields, their quiet paths through the trees.

Then he broke. He turned for the quickest of glances. Eurydice was there, looking at him, but only for the time it took her to begin to shake her head and begin to open her mouth in a silent cry. Then she was gone, and where she had stood there was only the mist drifting across the path. She faded down into the dark, already forgetting who Orpheus had been.

He would have followed her, but she had simply disappeared. He could not see her on the path back down, or higher up. Numb, he sat for hours at the side of the track, staring into space, and when finally he stumbled on upwards he no longer cared whether he reached the sunlight or not.

46

Notes

ANCIENT GREECE

Apollo (Say Ap-ol'-low) (p. 24-9)
Apollo was one of the Olympian gods. He was a son of Zeus, and the god of art, music, poetry, medicine and prophecy. The temple of Apollo at Delphi was one of the most famous temples in Greece. (See 'Olympus'.)

Athene (Say Ath-ee'-nee) (p. 5, 32-7)
Athene, sometimes spelled 'Athena', was the protectress of Athens. She was goddess of the crafts and arts of town life, especially weaving. Athene invented the flute, but gave it up when she saw it spoilt her appearance to blow it so hard. In paintings and sculptures, and in *The Odyssey*, she is portrayed as a beautiful woman in armour.

Dionysus (Say Die-on-eye'-sus) (p. 18-23)
Dionysus was the son of Zeus and Semele, a mortal. He was first the god of wine, then later he became a god of music and drama, and other pleasures. He was also associated with milk and honey, and feasting.

Gods (p. 4-5)
Gods were everywhere in Ancient Greece. For instance, every river had its own god. Sculptures and paintings showed them with human bodies, though often they were thought of as being much bigger than humans. Gods could change shape and were immortal. Gods and humans intermingled. Gods fell in love with human beings, and had children by them. They interfered in human lives, helping and hindering.

Hades (Say Hay'-dees) (p. 40-44)
Hades was the brother of Zeus and king of the Underworld, which included Tartarus, where evil-doers were punished, and the Elysian Fields, a place where the good and heroic lived after death. Hades stole Persephone from the world of the living to be his wife. She was thought to visit the upper world each spring to visit her mother, the goddess Demeter, and return to Hades in the autumn.

Hermes (Say Her'-mees) (p. 16)
Hermes was the gods' messenger and also the god of travellers, roads, merchants, luck and even thieving. By noon on the day of his birth he had invented the lyre, by evening he'd stolen cattle from Apollo. He had winged sandals, a wide hat and a staff with serpents twined round it. Small statues of Hermes often stood at the doors of houses.

Lyre (p. 25, 26, 38, 40, 44)
The lyre was a string instrument that was held in the hands and plucked. It was made from a tortoise shell which had two arms leading from it. The arms were joined by a cross bar, to which the strings were attached. When the strings were plucked, the tortoise shell would make the sound from them louder.

Nymphs (p. 30-32)
Nymphs were women who stayed young for about ten thousand years. There were nymphs of the sea, rivers,

streams, brooks, stagnant waters, mountainsides and trees. They could cure sick people and make prophecies, and they liked weaving and spinning. They were mainly helpful to humans, but some dragged men down into rivers.

Odysseus (Say Od-iss'-ee-us) (p. 6-17)
Odysseus was the most cunning chieftain of the Greeks during their war with Troy. *The Odyssey*, said to have been composed by the poet Homer, is the thrilling tale of Odysseus' long wanderings and adventures as he tried to get home after the end of the war. *The Odyssey* was sung by poets who learnt it by heart. It probably took more than one evening to hear right through.

Olympus (p. 34, 37)
The Greeks thought that Olympus, a mountain 3,000 m high in northern Greece, was the home of the gods. There were twelve main Olympians and many lesser gods. The chief of the Olympians was Zeus, who was married to his sister Hera.

Oracle (p. 40)
Oracles were the answers to the questions that people asked the gods at famous temples throughout Greece. The answers were interpreted by the priests and priestesses of the temples. They were often difficult to understand or misleading. At the oracle of Zeus at Dodona, the priest listened to the sound of oak leaves and interpreted their meaning.

Orpheus (Say Orf'-ee-us) (p. 38-46)
Orpheus was a famous musician. He was such a wonderful player of the lyre that wild creatures would stand spellbound, listening to him. He went on the expedition in the *Argo* to win the Golden Fleece, where his music put to sleep the serpent that guarded the fleece.

Pan (p. 4, 24-9)
Pan was a god of the countryside, the protector of shepherds and flocks. He had the lower body, horns and beard of a goat, and the head and upper body of a man. He played on a small reed pipe.

Poseidon (Say Pos-eye'-don) (p. 7, 36)
Poseidon was the brother of Zeus and was the chief god of the sea. He was called the Earthshaker. He helped to build Troy, but because he was not paid for the work, he helped the Greeks fight against the Trojans in the Trojan War. After the war, Poseidon turned against Odysseus because he blinded Poseidon's son Polyphemus, the Cyclops.

Silenus (Say Si-lee'-nus) (p. 18-21)
Silenus was the companion and the tutor of Dionysus. Sometimes he was called a god. He was always pictured as a fat, drunk old man, generally riding a donkey or an ass. He had great knowledge, and knew the past and the future.

Tantalus (p. 44)
Tantalus was a man who offended the gods, either by stealing nectar from them, or revealing their secrets, or by serving them with the flesh of his own son, Pelops, at a feast. He was condemned to suffer eternal punishment in Tartarus.

Zeus (Say Z-you'-ss) (p. 4, 5, 36)
Zeus was the chief of the Olympian gods. He drew lots with his brothers, Poseidon and Hades, to see which part of the world each should look after. Zeus drew the sky and the land it illuminated. He was the giver of laws to men, and the provider of justice. He was known for often falling in love with human women and would appear in disguise to trick them and, usually, force them to submit to him.

Further Reading

Ancient Greece (*Jump! History Books*) by Robert Nicholson and Claire Watts (Franklin Watts, 1991)
Gods and Men (*Myths and Legends from the World's Religions series*) retold by John Bailey, Kenneth McLeish, David Spearman (OUP, 1993)
Greek and Norse legends by Cheryl Evans, ill. by Rodney Matthews (Usborne, 1987)
Greek Myths and Legends by John Snelling (Wayland, 1987)

Perseus the gorgon-slayer by Jane O'Loughlin, ill. by Katharine Stafford (Keystone Picture Books) (Era Pubns, 1991)
The legend of Odysseus by Peter Connolly (OUP, 1986)
The Orchard Book of Greek Myths retold by Geraldine McCaughrean, ill. by Emma Chichester Clark (Orchard Books, 1993)